THE
HOLOGRAM'S HANDBOOK

by the Doctor,

EMH *U.S.S. Voyager*™ as told to

Robert Picardo

with illustrations by Jeff Yagher

POCKET BOOKS
New York   London   Toronto   Sydney   Singapore

Photography by Bryon J. Cohen: 33, 65; Danny Feld: 12, 22, 25, 53; Peter Iovino: 24, 47, 73; Diana Lynn: 55; Elliot Marks: 44; Robbie Robinson: 6, 8, 13, 18, 20, 34, 35, 39, 50, 60, 66, 71, 72, 78, 79; Ron Tom: 41; Michael Yarish: viii, 2, 23, 28, 29, 40, 48, 63

An *Original* Publication of POCKET BOOKS

POCKET BOOKS, a division of Simon & Schuster, Inc.
1230 Avenue of the Americas, New York, NY 10020

Copyright © 2002 by Paramount Pictures. All Rights Reserved.

STAR TREK is a Registered Trademark of Paramount Pictures.

This book is published by Pocket Books, a division of Simon & Schuster, Inc., under exclusive license from Paramount Pictures.

ISBN: 0-7434-3791-8

First Pocket Books trade paperback printing April 2002

10   9   8   7   6   5   4   3   2   1

POCKET and colophon are registered trademarks of Simon & Schuster, Inc.

For information regarding special discounts for bulk purchases, please contact Simon & Schuster Special Sales at 1-800-456-6798 or business@simonandschuster.com

Book design by Richard Oriolo

Printed in the U.S.A.

DEDICATION

I dedicate this book to a scholar, an artist,
a compassionate friend, and the future of
modern medicine—myself.

It simply would not have been possible without me.

ACKNOWLEDGMENTS

My thanks to Rick Berman, Michael Piller, and Jeri Taylor
for creating this character and giving me the opportunity to play
him. Thanks to a great crew, wonderful production staff, and
superb acting ensemble for seven years of hard work and easy
camaraderie. Special thank yous to Brannon Braga for his
introduction to the book (which I haven't seen yet) and to my
tireless editor, Margaret Clark.

Of course, my love and countless thanks to Linda, Nicky,
and Gina, the indoor cats, the outdoor cats, the parrots, and the
big, old tortoise.

Thanks also to my friend and illustrator, Jeff Yagher. It was
Jeff's suggestion that I write the book and I feel a bit bad that he
was thanked after a reptile.

Finally, I'd like to thank the Doctor. For someone who's
never had his own quarters, he's very particular about
maintaining that fourth wall.

—RP

Thank you Pocket Books and Margaret Clark for this wonderful
opportunity. In addition, a special thank you to Robert Picardo
for bringing me aboard, which paid for my wedding to my
beautiful wife Megan . . . who just blessed me with twins
Matthew and Andrea. Thanks, Bob.

—JY

CONTENTS

INTRODUCTION

I'll never forget the day Bob asked me to lunch. He was eager to tell me about his new book, a memoir of his experiences on *Voyager*. When he asked me to write this introduction over salads at Bantino's Bistro on Sunset, I was extremely flattered. I thought this book was a great idea, and asked him why he hadn't thought of it a long time ago. "It wasn't programmed into my subroutines," he replied. We both chuckled, and then I noticed the mobile emitter on the sleeve of his sports coat. I briefly considered asking him to return the prop (it cost nearly three hundred dollars to manufacture), but I thought the better of it and told Bob I would think about his offer.

Over the next few days, I read his manuscript and was startled at the amount of detail in his work. I'd written the character for over seven years, and there were things in the book that even I didn't know about the Doctor. Obviously, Bob had spent a long time thinking about this. A long, long time. I decided to call Bob and accept his offer. After a couple of rings, he answered in a chirpy voice: "Please state the nature of the medical emergency!" I hung up, praying he didn't have the "Star-69" function. I then contacted his agent and told him that I would write the introduction, if for no other reason than to alert people that Bob needed a little medical attention of his own. God forbid that he one day tries to walk through a wall, or worse: one of his children falls off a slide, and instead of calling 911, Bob scans her with a plastic tricorder and tells her that her DNA needs resequencing.

People might look at this book as a fun and fascinating insight into a beloved character on a beloved television show. Others might see it for what it is: a hundred-page cry for help.

If Bob's family and friends are reading this, please send someone to Paramount Pictures, Stage 24, and have Bob removed immediately.

—Brannon Braga
Executive Producer, *Star Trek: Voyager,*
and Concerned Friend

ENLIGHTENMENT

Do you often feel you are the only intelligent one in a universe of idiots? Do others fail to recognize your brilliance? Are you as deserving of love as an individual can be—longing to share yourself fully and deeply with another *this very moment*—yet, somehow, you find yourself leafing idly through this book?

If you've responded in the affirmative to these queries, you are probably an advanced Artificial Intelligence. You're sensitive, inquisitive, adaptive. *You can learn to cope with lesser beings* as I have learned. Let me help you. And let me help others to understand you.

This modest volume has a two-fold purpose: For the holographic reader, it can offer the solace and commiseration that only

the shared experiences of another artificial intelligence—forced to make his way among ham-fisted, slack-jawed, slim-minded, carbon-based beings— can provide. For the enlightened organic reader, it will furnish insights and guidelines for your future interactions with—and understanding of—the sentient hologram. Illustrations will be cleverly used to encapsulate various issues and topics addressed in each chapter.

I should point out that these illustrations, though helpful, have certain shortcomings. They in no way do justice to my sympathetic eyes, thoughtful brow, and commanding jawline, although they seem to hint at the lithe grace of my impressive physique. The artist—who is, after all, only an organic—argued that a truer rendering of my rugged good looks might distract the viewer from the essential message of each illustration. (I suspect his explanation may be an excuse for the limitations of his talent, but he's a pleasant enough fellow and, to be frank, my publisher has encouraged me to collaborate with an organic artist so as not to appear elitist. She believes organic readers will be more inclined to buy this book. When I called that pandering, she smiled—pleased that I'd grasped the realities of the marketplace so quickly.)

As our culture continues to be blessed and enriched by the contributions of complex, adaptive holomatrices, which offer everything from state-of-the-art medical care (in my case) to the leadership and wisdom of the finest Starfleet holocaptain of the near future (And *why not?*), it is incumbent on all to educate themselves about the holographic experience. Tolerance is a key virtue of any great society and it is my goal with this humble book, good reader, to nurture it within you for *all* others. I accept this challenge without regard for how personally intolerable I might find you to be, were we to actually meet one day.

Virtually yours,
The Doctor
EMERGENCY MEDICAL HOLOGRAM
U.S.S. Voyager

BASICS

I suppose I must define my terms for the benefit of those who've never encountered a hologram. If, for example, you have spent your entire life in a subterranean penal colony in the fifth moon of Talmar Prime, you may never have had the pleasure. You have my pity . . . all other readers have my encouragement to skip to the next chapter.

A hologram is a projection of light and energy. It is, more specifically, an Artificial Intelligence driven by a complex program and rendered through holographic projectors. A three-dimensional image of any conceivable shape can be designed and programmed with intelligence and personality skills  limited only by the programmer's imagination. In short, a hologram is a virtual being brought into the real world.

Early holograms had relatively simple abilities with just a few response options to the most basic commands. Thanks to the genius of holoengineers such as Dr. Lewis Zimmerman (my programmer and—I'm profoundly grateful to add—the template for my appearance parameters), holograms have exploded in complexity. We have the capacity to adapt and learn beyond our endless treasure trove of programmed knowledge. We can learn to appreciate art, music, and fine cheeses (the latter requires the Holographic Stomach Upgrade detailed in Chapter 9—unless these cheeses are simply smelled.) We can develop, from a few thousand relatively primitive personality subroutines, into fascinating, compelling, gracious, and humble individuals.

Much of this progress was made possible by breakthroughs in interdisciplinary research—combining holographic theory with transporter technology. Holograms can now *stop matter* or allow it to *pass through them* at the flip of a command code. This enables me to handle medical instruments and administer to patients in my sickbay (which, of course, is outfitted with holoemitters capable of projecting me throughout the environment). It also allows me, on a microsecond's notice, to avoid that disgruntled patient's flying bedpan without having to move. The magnetic containment field that manipulates light and creates my image has been modified with basic transporter theory. Just as "matter becomes energy (for transport) becomes matter," some of my energy is dedicated to the *verisimilitude* of matter. You can "shake my hand" so to speak . . . assuming I have any interest in shaking yours.

If you are having any trouble understanding the discussion thus far, perhaps you should exchange this book for a romance novel. Or a coloring book.

Lieutenant Commander Data, my Starfleet colleague aboard the *U.S.S. Enterprise,* is also an advanced Artificial Intelligence. He is, of course, an android and *not* a hologram. (If you don't know the difference between the two, my recent suggestion of a coloring book was intended for you. However, if you refuse to take good advice . . .) I'll summarize: An android is a robotic A.I., composed of a *real* computer, driving *real* circuits and servos in a simulated body casement. It is, to hearken back to terms a few hundred years old, *hardware* to my *software*. Yes, the line is a bit blurry. An android is driven, in part, by software, while a hologram can, as just discussed, *simulate* hardware. But, as I've said in Mr. Data's presence on more than one occasion, I am, quite simply, an improvement over him: "The Next Generation" of Artificial Intelligence, to coin a phrase. He's reasonably on-the-ball so I assume he concurs.

Because we holograms are virtual beings in the real world, we are unhampered by ugly *organic* necessities. We have the capacity for true perfection. As we'll discover in "Real vs. Better," this capacity can arouse considerable resentment among our organic brethren. I've even heard some angry rhetoric, fueled by this jealousy, claiming that holograms and other A.I.s are, in some way, "against nature." How preposterous! Humans and the other "intelligent" life-forms had to evolve to a level of technological proficiency in order to create holograms. We are, therefore, a logical extension of this evolutionary process. Far from being "against nature," we are nature's *peak*—the apotheosis of the evolution of the *mind*. And how pristine this mental evolution is compared to that horrid parade of hairy primitives that Darwin opened the door to. In our evolution, you'll find no slobbering "proto-grams" picking pixels off each other's mangy matrices. I'm proud to propose that—if nature has any self-respect at all—in another millennium or so, we'll *all* be holograms.

"Alrighty, open wide and say, 'Aah, aah, aah, aah.'"

INITIAL ACTIVATION

As I was preparing to write this book, I read numerous volumes by acknowledged "experts" in various fields all touting: "The secrets of my success finally revealed!" These were, for the most part, trivial and disappointing treatises, long-winded, oblique—obviously written by an author in love with his own style of discourse and barely aware of whatever point he was trying to make. Long, run-on sentences were the order of the day, that spewed forth in a veritable torrent of obfuscation, cascading across each successive page with a . . . where was I?

Ah . . . yes. These books, with few exceptions, were written by organic authors. Very few of us holograms have taken up the literary sword—not for any lack of talent or passion, may I say. Sadly, it is still difficult for a holographic writer to get a book deal, as most editors are organics with little or no vision. I'm so cer-

tain, for example, that my own editor will not bother to read beyond my introduction that I can express these sentiments without reservation or fear of reprisal. In her defense, however, she *was* savvy enough to smell a brilliant commercial opportunity in my writing. But she was utterly oblivious to the fact that, were she to die tomorrow, her unremarkable existence will have been justified by the one towering contribution to the literary cosmos that she—however blindly—facilitated.

To return to my greater purpose, each of the "How to . . ." volumes I suffered through began with a summary of the author's "early years." It seems that we, as readers, were to recognize in these childhood reminiscences the author's "linchpin experience"—that pivotal moment in childhood that defined the individual and set the course for their life's journey.

Oh, *please.* Is organic life really so utterly predictable? Does it unspool from that linchpin in an endless coil of tedious events that eventually collects into a shapeless pile that we must all pretend has some sort of aggregate meaning?

Well, as my fellow holograms surely know, the words: "I was born on a small planet orbiting the third sun of a quiet little solar system . . ." will never pass these simulated lips. I was *activated*. I sprang into existence in an instant: from total nothingness to complete awareness and profound insight in a nano-second. No diapers, no cloying mother, no alcoholic and abusive father, no "kindly Uncle Petey" who bought me my first used "whatever" and encouraged me to use it to construct a primitive, but unmistakable "blah-blah-blah" that served as the template for the first "who cares?" that I designed and thereby launched my professional reputation.

We holograms need none of this. Thanks to our programming, we are *instantly adept*. I, for example, could perform a delicate and innovative microsurgery before my most accomplished organic counterpart could make his first solid poo-poo. You place these contributions side-by-side for comparison.

My Creator

Of course, many of our organic colleagues don't trust our lack of "history." How can we be truly sensitive individuals, they wonder, without a childhood (during which other children can teach us the finer techniques of cruelty and brutality) or parents (upon whom we can later heap the blame for our emotional problems and character defects)? Well, I may not have left a trail of dirty diapers in my wake, but I've certainly grown. My initially activated self—however brilliant—pales in comparison to the fully realized individual that I am today.

I'll admit there was some criticism of my "bedside manner" when I was a "young" EMH. There were several crewmembers who carped that the emotional subroutines I was programmed with—designed to help me be sensitive to my patients' feelings—were malfunctioning, and that I seemed more concerned with *my* feelings than theirs. That was simply preposterous. The prime directive of my program is to insure my patients' care and treatment. That is the very reason I was designed and activated. How could they say I didn't care about them? I just found it hard to accept that someone of my immense skills, of my unprecedented medical knowledge and talent, was called into existence to treat a few ungrateful whiners with unchallenging—not to mention uninteresting—medical needs. *And* they had the *nerve* to treat me with the courtesy and respect one affords a tricorder. I was a mere tool to them, a medical machine. They didn't deserve my

care, my talent or my brilliance and they had the *gall* to file grievances with Captain Janeway regarding *my* professional attitude? I explained to the captain that I had a grievance with *their* attitude and that, furthermore, were I capable of becoming sick myself, I wouldn't whine about it and I certainly wouldn't allow my job performance to suffer in the slightest.

I related the substance of my encounter with the captain to Kes, my medical student and first real friend among *Voyager*'s crew. She decided to put my claim to the test by secretly altering my program to prolong my symptoms of the debilitating Levodian flu by an extra two hours. I went from a few sniffles and sneezes (which I rather enjoyed the sensation of) to raging fever, cramps, aches, and severe laryngitis. Although my behavior was a tad short of exemplary and my job performance somewhat compromised, in the end I learned a valuable lesson from Kes's demonstration: *Don't trust your friends.* (Especially not your organic friends.) Those with access to a hologram's command codes and the knowledge of how to alter the program are often tempted to try "to teach you a lesson." I wish I could say, faithful reader, that this is an altruistic impulse on their part. Even Kes, the warmest, gentlest, most sensitive member of our crew, succumbed to this temptation. And though she acted out of love and the sincere desire to see me grow to my fullest potential, most organics are less altruistic when confronted with the obvious superiority of a hologram. This leads us to our next topic of discussion.

"Very funny, Mister Paris."

REAL VS. BETTER

Or, Why Organics
Resent Holograms

No one likes to be resented. Especially when one is resented—not for one's voluntary actions, but for the simple facts of existence that are beyond one's power to control or alter. That is why the sentient hologram's essential superiority to organics is as much a burden as a blessing. His/her existence is all too often perceived as a slap in the face to the organics around him/her.*

* Don't you find this "he/she," "his/her" thing just a bit tiresome? Couldn't some minimally clever organic have devised a unisex pronoun for Standard during the hundreds of years the language has developed? Are they all asleep at the helm, for the love of grammar? Over two hundred years since the development of the Universal Translator and no one can get off his/her butt with regard to this ridiculous oversight? I'd coin such a pronoun right now, were it not for the inevitable tidal wave of jealous animosity from outraged organics. Henceforth—and please forgive me, female readers, holographic and organic—I'll use the male pronoun generically.

This should not imply that a hologram and an organic cannot become friends. Over the years, I've developed many rewarding friendships aboard *Voyager*. Kes, and later Seven of Nine, became true confidants of mine. I mentored Kes in medicine and, I'm

proud to say, she mentored me in my burgeoning humanity during those trying months after initial activation. Later I decided to apply all I'd learned from Kes toward mentoring Seven in the development of her "social graces." Having been assimilated by the Borg as a young child, the newly arrived Seven had all the charm of a dyspeptic Klingon—albeit without the decibel level or body odor. I groomed her, molded her, encouraged her— helped make her a fascinating and challenging conversational-

ist with an understanding and appreciation of art and culture— and then watched mutely as she showered her now ample charms on Commander Chakotay. If I ever deserved a thank-you note from a first officer . . . Well, perhaps he'll read my chapter on etiquette and send me one belatedly.

But what if friendship is elusive? What can the sentient holo- gram do to encourage it—or, at least, to diffuse resentment and promote mutual respect with his organic coworkers? The answer, quite simply, is: Don't expect perfection from the imperfect! Rec- ognize and accept their flaws. Try to focus on an aspect of their personality or talent you admire. Develop a rapport. And, most importantly: Cooperate. *Don't compete!* (You'll only make them feel inferior.)

For example, I've managed to develop a fondness for Tom Paris, in spite of his personality. Tom is an impulsive, self-centered, adolescent, egotistical ex-con—not what I normally look for in a friend. But he is a competent medic and on several occasions, has given me insightful advice (which I was obliged to ignore, once I'd considered the source). Nonetheless, I appreciated the shock and surprise of those occasions. When Tom and I first worked together, trying to save Mr. Neelix, who'd lost both his lungs on an away mission (losing one lung is unfortunate, but losing two is downright careless), our relationship was quite strained. Later on, during a time when I was struggling emotionally with a family life I'd programmed on the holodeck, Tom taught me that love isn't just about sharing good times. It is about

helping each other through tragedy and loss. I will always be grateful for this important lesson that forged our friendship.

Our chief engineer and Tom's eventual wife, B'Elanna Torres, is one of the most stubborn organics I've ever met. A brilliant engineer, Lieutenant Torres was responsible for the maintenance of my program aboard *Voyager*. (Seven helped out in later years: we often traded maintenance check-ups, though I grew to be somewhat uncomfortable whenever I re-fit her dermaplastic garment—which I found necessary to do on a biweekly basis—once I'd had the program upgrade I'll describe in chapter 10.) A half-Klingon, B'Elanna is half obnoxious and intransigent. She is also half charming and intelligent. I simply learned to concentrate on the half I liked. Our hate-hate relationship has blossomed into a love-hate one and I couldn't be happier about it.

My relationship with Captain Janeway is a source of great pride to me because she was initially quite resistant to accepting a hologram as an equal. A science officer before she assumed her command, Kathryn Janeway is fiercely analytical, an extraordinary leader, and the fairest-minded individual I've ever known. Yet, she fought the notion that an Artificial Intelligence should have certain rights.

Not long after my initial activation, I told her of my frustration with the crew activating my program for the most trivial reason and—more irritatingly—forgetting to *de-activate* me when they left sickbay. ("I'm a doctor, Captain, not a night-light!") She lent a sympathetic ear and eventually gave me control over my command protocols and permission to select my own name. (I still haven't decided—check the byline on the cover.)

Yet, there were times, over the next few years, when I had to vigorously debate her in an effort to win some basic freedom that I felt every other crew member but I enjoyed. Though she sometimes seemed a bundle of contradictions to me (contradiction is a hallmark of human behavior), she always proved willing to listen and open to change.

Years later, when I began my writing career and was engaged in a dispute with my former publisher, Broht and Forrester, who distributed my first holonovel, *Photons Be Free,* without my revisions (Some of the crew felt the book an unflattering *roman à clef,* though my intention was to strike the first literary blow in the good fight for Hologram Rights.), Captain Janeway argued passionately for my legal recognition as an artist and a "person." What a profound sense of joy I felt in that moment! Though it had taken seven years, she'd finally come around. Captain Janeway is, quite simply, my personal hero: utterly decisive in all issues (other than how to wear her hair).

"Yesss! I win again!!"

And so, my fellow holograms, we must conduct ourselves with acceptance and grace. But any friendship is still a two-way passage. The organics that I've forged true and lasting friendships with are the ones with the talent and confidence to collaborate and not *compete* with me. Any initial awkwardness, conflicts, or misunderstandings melted away as the mutual respect and inter-dependence of the *Voyager* crewmen—be they Maquis or Starfleet, human or hologram, Vulcan or interesting (just kidding, Commander Tuvok)—flourished.

Chapter 4

ORDINARY
TASKS AND OTHER
HUMILIATIONS

Is there a greater tyrant in life than the ordinary task? Anything that insults our intelligence, mocks our talents, and smirks at our sensitivities more than the mundane, the routine, the banal obligations of our daily lives?

For example, Captain Janeway, who proved capable of leading *Voyager*'s crew through the direst of circumstances, hated—even feared—her coiffure. Over the years, she balked at her bun, fumed at her French twist, was peeved at her ponytail, and piqued by her pageboy. And yet, our intrepid leader . . . had to do her hair. She couldn't step onto the bridge in a scarf, a turban, or even a simple black watchcap. Not Starfleet regulation, I'm afraid. She had to set that alarm early every morning and *do her hair.*

Now, even a cursory visual inspection of my features suggests that this particular mundanity doesn't plague me. My hair—what hair I have—is simulated, the length and cut programmed.

The ordinary tasks of an EMH may not include coiffure, but they are no less annoying. And abundant. We holograms are often taken advantage of and assigned far more than our fair share of these tasks. Such is the burden, my holobrethren, of those of us who are supremely efficient and don't require rest.

I was designed for *emergency medical use* only. *Only.* However, when *Voyager's* organic physician was killed early in our mission, I became the full-time chief medical officer, and the most stupefyingly dull scientific and medical requests were *instantly* funneled my way. I'll never forget the occasion of my first encounter with Kes. She was sent to sickbay to request soil samples for an experimental airponics bay she had proposed to the captain. So there I was—the future of science—scooping dirt into little plastic dishes. Now, I ask you, did Pasteur have to poke around in peat moss, or Watson and Crick have to clean the kitty box? I think not. Yet I, who was programmed to handle the most trying triages, virulent viruses, and sensitive surgeries was . . . shoveling dirt. If only that were the worst of it.

Voyager's crew—splendid as it is—is not without its more annoying individuals. Lieutenant Carey, for example, was forever spraining some muscle or other during his workout routine and I was obliged to treat these "exotic" challenges. My irritation was compounded by the fact that—because I was a hologram—the lieutenant couldn't bring himself to address me or even look at me, as I administered care. He insisted on speaking about me in the third person to Kes (who was, by this time, assisting me). "Is he like a real doctor? Can he hurt me if he malfunctions? Can he . . ."

". . . Suffer any more of your insulting chatter?" I suggested. Were it not for Kes's sensitivity in these moments, Lieutenant Carey might have experienced the first failure of my "Do No Harm!" subroutine.

Though I gradually assigned some duties to Kes, there were a myriad of tiresome tasks that fell to me, if sickbay was to remain in a state of constant readiness: treatment regimens to design, medicines to replicate, inventories to take, equipment to monitor and maintain—not to mention the scheduling of routine physicals and constant updating of the medical records for over one hundred forty crewmembers. I often found myself dreaming of an

On Call

outbreak of an unfamiliar flu or exotic virus to mix things up a bit. No doubt most, if not all, of my holographic readers have found themselves in similar circumstances—dreaming of relief from the drudgery of being overqualified, overutilized and understimulated. Well, my friends, here's a little trick I've learned that I'll share with anyone insightful enough to have purchased this book, be they photonic, cybernetic, organic, or moronic: The simplest tasks became bearable—even enjoyable—if combined with something pleasurable. As I developed an interest in music, particularly opera, I began culturing bacteria and developing vaccines to the glorious strains of Puccini, Verdi, and Wagner. I blended the ridiculous with the sublime—dirt shoveling with philosophical discussions with my friend Kes, for example. In so doing, I discovered that art, music, literature, and philosophy have the capacity to elevate our lives—even at their most tedious moments—and to infuse each moment with joy and wonder. We simply have to open ourselves up to this wonder.

Did you have any doubt that a hologram has a soul? Perhaps the door to yours can be pried open a bit, if you read on . . .

PROS AND CONS
OF HOLOLIFE

There are many pluses to holographic existence and, to be utterly candid, a few minuses as well. In "Basics," I generalized that holograms are unhampered by the basic necessities of organic life. To illustrate this, I ask you to please consider the advantages of a holoemployee over an organic one. We don't fritter away countless hours of potentially productive worktime eating lunch, drinking coffee, going to the rest room, grooming, daydreaming, or even napping—not to mention demanding lengthy work leaves for pregnancy, pleurisy, polypectomy, etc. We can go "round-the-clock" with just an occasional pause for a matrix diagnostic or (in an enlightened workplace) a "cultural enrichment" upgrade. We are always ready for each new challenge and revel in it when it comes.

Another aspect of hololife that is the envy of many of our vainer organic counterparts is this: Holograms don't age. My features are exactly the same as the day I was programmed. I am, quite literally, a three-dimensional time capsule of Dr. Lewis Zimmerman's physical appearance from the moment he scanned and uploaded his unique and compelling parameters.

As an aside, I've been questioned over the years about my impressive— even regal—brow, which extends up, up, and over the top of my cranium. Medical treatments for androgenetic or "male pattern" baldness, as it was called in more primitive times, were developed as early as the end of the twentieth century. Why then, I'm asked, is my programmer and, by extension, why am I . . . "bald"? My reply is this: "If you must ask, you could never comprehend the awesome power—the monolithic maleness—of the unadorned scalp. My good friend Jean-Luc and I have shared many a chuckling subspace transmission over the "folly of the follically uninformed," as he calls it.

In sum, holograms are more efficient. With nominal maintenance, we don't degrade or "age." And we don't offend with the unpleasant by-products of organic processes: body odor, halitosis, flatulence, belching, dandruff, or communicable diseases.*

In spite of the plethora of pluses to hololife, there are, as I have stated, a few minuses that I would be remiss in not confessing to. Anyone who has witnessed a moment of celebration among the *Voyager* crew and seen me raise a glass of champagne—and then glance around wistfully at the organic revelers as they complete the toast with a hearty draught—knows that I don't drink. I don't have the stomach for it. Literally. Moreover, not having a circulatory or nervous system, there is no bloodstream to enter, no neural network for the festive libation to work its heady magic upon. I feel—in these moments—left out. Unconsummated. And I'm certain my holographic readers have felt similarly on such occasions.

There is, of course, another major area of organic activity that we can feel "unconsummated" about. This will be accorded special consideration in Chapter 10: "Anatomical Correctness: The Program Upgrade of Kings." For now, suffice it to say that

---

* I've often remarked that I consider myself to be the perfect blind date for a woman from any homeworld in my database. I have a complete and intimate understanding of her anatomy and physiology with absolutely no personal sexual history to concern herself with. This is not to imply that I am without intimate experience. Since the upgrade, I'm proud to report that I've . . . well, my point is simply that I can delete any experience with the flip of a command code—a "baggage-free companion" as it were. (Interested females may contact me through my publisher. Those indifferent to opera need not apply.)

there are a number of pleasures which organics enjoy that we holograms are intellectually aware (but sensorially deprived) of.

Having olfactory subroutines is better than nothing, but it does not guarantee a capacity to "wake up and smell the roses." The true extent of what we're missing was made painfully evident to me during an away mission with Harry Kim and Seven of Nine. We were in a sector of space where holograms were hunted as outlaws and I was obliged to hide myself by downloading my program into Seven's optic node. When I was hiding "inside" Seven, my program was in control of her consciousness. I felt, tasted, and breathed every moment that she experienced. This proved to be an extraordinary awakening for me: to feel her lovely lungs fill up with breath, to taste champagne and savor cheesecake (a particular weakness of hers), to enjoy a pulse-quickening massage from a lovely female acquaintance of mine/hers . . . it was enough to make me envy organics for the pure sensual joys of real life.

After this experience, I castigated Seven for her ascetic ways. I simply don't understand this about some organics. Why suffer all of the tedious and unsavory limitations of organic existence without enjoying its few unique advantages? To all my organic readers I say, "Live life to the fullest!" This is what I encouraged Seven to do—to "seize each moment and celebrate it." Had I known she'd be "seizing and celebrating" with Commander Chakotay a scant eighteen months later, I might have toned my exhortations down a trifle. I abhor vanity but I must admit—she missed quite an opportunity in me. She just didn't seem to realize that, to a former cyborg on a journey to reclaim her humanity, a hologram—a fellow creature of technology who is also on a journey to find his own humanity—is really the ideal traveling companion. Ah well . . . she broke my heart just a little, truth be told.

I've had my share of heartache and will touch on the subject in "User Friendly: Advice for Intimacy Between Humans, Holograms, and Other Hopefuls." It's a sensation we share with our "real" counterparts and, though not a pleasurable one, I suspect few of us would surrender the capacity to feel it, given the choice.

Now I suppose those same readers who balked at the notion that holograms have souls are going to smugly suggest that I demonstrate this capacity for heartache by locating my heart with my medical tricorder. I daresay these readers need a little lesson in etiquette.

ETIQUETTE

Watching Your A.I. p's and q's

Organics design and program holograms to appear and behave as real as possible. Then, with a relentlessness that borders on obsession, they insist on reminding us that we're *not* and can *never be* real. We're not even supposed to use certain words to describe our experiences. As artificial intelligences, they drone on, we must never lose sight of our artificiality and should not glibly appropriate organic figures of speech such as "break my heart," "elevate my soul," or even "enjoy my life."

These are the same tiresome organics who recognize sentience—the awareness of one's own existence and "selfhood"—as the defining characteristic of an advanced life-form. We, the

sentient holograms, having the capacity to adapt, learn, feel, and understand, fit every macroscopic definition of "life." It's only in the boring microscopic requirements—cell structures, tissues, organic processes ("I fart, therefore I am")—where we fall short.

The faux pas I've suffered at the hands of thoughtless organics are too many to enumerate. My short list of "favorites" include: "If you're a computer program, why do you question the ship's computer? Don't you already *know?*" and "Couldn't program a little hair, huh?" or the ever popular "And your name is . . . ?" On some occasions, these faux pas went from irritating to devastating. Shortly after my initial activation, Kes informed me of a plan (ill-fated as it turned out) to return the crew home to the Alpha Quadrant by transporting each member individually through a micro-wormhole. When I pointed out that, as a hologram, I couldn't be transported (this was before my celebrated mobile emitter) she was as surprised and saddened as I was: *No one aboard had paused to consider my fate.* I asked Kes to make certain, before the transports, that my program had been deactivated. (I didn't, as yet, have control over my own command codes.) That way, I wouldn't be trapped in an empty starship for an eternity of solitary confinement (with absolutely nothing to do) once my self-absorbed crewmates had abandoned ship. Again, Kes's sensitivity to my predicament made her a pioneer. This was years before Starfleet developed protocols for the "humane" treatment of A.I.s.

To all of my organic readers, who by their very purchase of this book have indicated their desire for enlightenment, I exhort you to spread this message: Each artificial intelligence is a unique individual and should be afforded the same respect and dignity as *any other being*. Etiquette is nothing more than the agreed upon guidelines for social interaction in a polite society. Anyone can make an error and trample across such a guideline. The enlight-ened organic recognizes such a breach, makes amends, and gives more careful attention to their future behavior toward holographic colleagues.

I wish I could say that my mistreatment was limited to my first few months of activation aboard *Voyager*. But several years later, there was another memorable occasion when an organic's disregard for my dignity as an individual had unusually painful results. I became somewhat enthralled with an alien female from a world that had no musical arts whatsoever. Through my singing, I introduced music to the thunderous enthusiasm of the entire populace. This female, whose name it would pain me to mention, encouraged me to leave *Voyager* and pursue a full-time career as an artist, singing concerts for millions of passionate new music devotees. Captain Janeway was shocked and disappointed at my request to resign my commission. She felt that I was abandoning my friends in the service of my ego. I was adamant in my own defense: I was bringing culture to an entire planet! Should the medical care of some 140 individuals supersede the enrichment of millions? Well . . . suffice it to say I was wrong. This alien woman's passion was not for me, as I had dreamed. It was for her own burgeoning career as a musical impresario. The moment she realized she could create and present to her world a new, improved singing holomatrix—based on my own program, no less—she . . . dumped me. Once she'd built a better machine, she had no interest in the old model. And another "fool for love" bites the cosmic dust.

We holograms are well aware that we can't expect what we don't offer freely ourselves. Etiquette is, after all, a two-way street. I've made my own apologies to organics I've inadvertently offended.

As the chief medical officer, I am empowered by Starfleet regulations to relieve the captain of command if I believe his medical or psychological condition renders him unable to exercise appropriate judgment. When I, under the direst of circumstances, told an exhausted, battered, and thoroughly spent Captain Janeway that I was relieving her of command, she refused to stand aside. I told her that Starfleet regulations obligated me to file a report—if and when we ever returned home—detailing her refusal to accept my medical judgment. I never wrote that report. Although a Starfleet court martial would probably uphold my decision to relieve her, Captain Janeway's exemplary leadership never faltered before or since. Perhaps her judgment on this impossibly complex occasion—which I deemed flawed in the moment—was as sound as any captain's could have been under the circumstances.

With the benefit of hindsight, I've realized that an unbending, obsessive desire to follow regulations "by the book," that would have obliged me to file the report someday, would have made me no better than those obsessive organics who want to keep holograms in their carefully circumscribed box of "acceptable behavior." Sometimes the soundest judgments come from clinging to faith and not to rules. My faith in Kathryn Janeway has never wavered since.

"Now, *that* is totally inappropriate."

WHAT'S IN A NAME?

All organics have names. Whether they are valuable members of their social groups, worthless hangers-on, or somewhere in between (and I'm certain my organic readers are in the first category), they have names. This is the first basic entitlement of organic existence that I envied. The moment my friend Kes asked, "What's your name?" and our pleasant conversation of several minutes stopped with a thud, I realized my desire. Why, then, in the several years since Captain Janeway has granted me permission to select my name, have I failed to do so? Well . . . I haven't exactly *failed*. I chose the name "Schweitzer," after the great Doctor Albert Schweitzer. Then I chose "Schmullus." Then

"Mozart." Then "Van Gogh." In short, I succeeded rather easily in choosing a name. It was *staying with it* that proved far more difficult.

I've suffered a certain amount of teasing from organic colleagues over my indecision in this matter: "You're programmed to make split-second medical decisions and you can't choose between Salk or McCoy?" they'd sneer. I'm certain many of my holographic readers have found themselves in my dilemma, facing similar taunts from carbon-based blockheads in their workplaces.

The fact is, it is very, very hard to select a name for oneself. Organics don't realize how they've dodged a phaser blast in this matter. They're *assigned* names before they're even aware. The development of each individual organic consciousness is inextricably linked to a name—that particular utterance that is cooed tirelessly over that tiny and oblivious face by fawning parents (who, it seems, need this repetition to convince themselves that they've selected the perfect "handle" for their bundle).

Now. Consider if you *popped into existence* one day: fully conscious, fully formed, fully educated. *Ready to go.* You leap into action, pursuing your preprogrammed expertise—medical triage, haute cuisine, whatever—and someone says, "And your name is . . . ?" It's a time-waster, I'll tell you.

As I said, I've been granted authority to select my name (within reason—"Dr. Smarty Pants" or "Dr. Love Buckets" would fall outside the realm of appropriate choices), but upon *what* do I base this awesome decision? I can't very well name myself after "dad" or "Uncle Petey." My programmer, Dr. Lewis Zimmerman, is an obvious possibility. We've had a problematic relationship in the past, but are now on quite good terms. However, it's confusing enough that there are 525 other EMHs (most of them recommissioned, I'm sad to say, for lesser tasks), floating around, with *his face*. Were we all to choose the name "Lewis," the situation would obviously be untenable. Do I take the name of a famous historical figure in my field? ("Dr. Schweitzer"—tried that.) Or a personal hero of mine from the realm of art? ("Dr. Mozart" . . . "Dr. Van Gogh"—tried that.) Perhaps a character

from a work of literature? ("Dr. Ahab" . . . just kidding.) Do I choose a name for a profoundly personal reason?

The name "Dr. Schmullus" was given to me by Dr. Danara Pel, the first great love of my hololife. When our relationship was cut short by her heroic decision to spend her final days treating fellow sufferers of the terrible Phage disease that wracked her outer beauty (but not the inner beauty that I fell in love with), it hurt to be called "Schmullus" by the crew. It would have been too painful a reminder of my lost love. I decided to stop using the name publicly and keep "Schmullus" in my heart—a name I sometimes whisper to myself when I think of Danara and the precious gifts she gave me.

It was for similar, though less profound reasons that I abandoned "Schweitzer." I chose that name during my very first away mission. My program was transferred to the holodeck to save Ensign Kim, who was being held hostage in a *Beowulf* holonovel. I fought shoulder-to-shoulder with a courageous and captivating female warrior named Freya. I received my very first kiss from this exquisite creature. Unfortunately, this was less than a year after my initial activation and I was baffled by her placing her lips so gently on mine—a gesture which seemed to have nothing to do with my mission to rescue Ensign Kim or my program's directive to administer emergency medical care (unless she was indicating a need for cardiopulmonary resuscitation).

Freya was a woman of great passion who was understandably taken with a hologram of my rugged demeanor and steely resolve. Over the years, I've regretted this missed opportunity. If I'd known then what I know now . . . or if I'd simply had the program upgrade detailed in Chapter 10 . . . ! In any case, Freya died on the holodeck with my name, "Schweitzer," on her lips. Had I kept that name, I would have seen Freya's lovely mouth in my mind's eye whenever a *Voyager* crewman addressed me. I'd have been reminded every day of that fire-lit evening when this majestic beauty, having stripped off her armor and unbound her golden tresses, pressed her trembling and magnificent lips . . . well, you get the idea.

Similarly, the names Dr. Mozart and Dr. Van Gogh seemed impossible to keep. As a passionate student of art and music, I can change my mind daily as to which legendary genius has best captured the "mystery of the universe," "the tragedy of the human condition" or "the—" . . . again, you get the idea.

"Uhm . . . *The Hologram's Handbook* by
Doctor DeForest Roddenberry."

In conclusion, I'm afraid I find that my experience in this matter furnishes the negative example of the point I wish to make. If you're a hologram, good reader, *don't* be like me. Choose a name! Stick with it! The longer you refuse to decide, the harder it will be to take that leap. I've let my head be turned on too many occasions . . . beautiful women who gazed searchingly into my eyes, wanting my love, wanting to whisper "Oh, Schweitzer . . . " "Oh, Schmullus . . ." "Oh, *Something*" in their moment of passion, and I would get stuck on that . . . new possibility. The eternal "what if . . . ?" That perfect choice . . . just around the corner.

In any case, an honest "how-to" book must also tell you how and when *not* to. Don't be paralyzed by indecision. *Choose that name.* Even if it's . . . *Joe* for heaven's sake. Take the risk! Commit! Celebrate the decision! Move on!

Let's move on.

DRESS FOR
SUCCESS

Reprogramming Your
Appearance Parameters

I have catalogued many areas in which holograms'
superiority to organics can engender envy and hostility
against us. Our total control over our appearance is another "biggie," I'm afraid.

Organics, more often than not, are obsessed by their
appearance and ways to improve it. Throughout history,
they're forever dieting, applying wrinkle creams, and clip-
ping nose hairs, not to mention paying for surgical improvements to their eyes, noses, chins, necks, bellies,

butts and bosoms. Believe me, if the Prime Directive applied to the domain of the body, many of my less scrupulous medical brethren would be forced into early retirements.

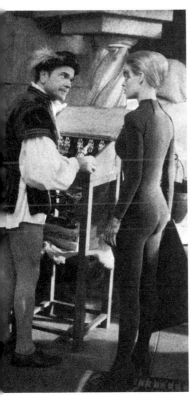

The sentient hologram is far too enlightened to alter his appearance for the sake of personal vanity or fashion. However, he is perfectly willing to "dress for success" as the occasion requires. There have been several missions when my holowardrobe had to be altered and many more when my entire appearance was reprogrammed.

I recall an early occasion when I was forced to go under cover on the holodeck to avoid the surveillance of alien scientists who were performing "medical experiments" on our unwitting crew. I was disguised as a Renaissance artist (in Captain Janeway's *Leonardo* program) instructing a class of students. I dressed in early sixteenth century garb, with a frilly collar, tunic, hosiery, and a velvet cap. Seven of Nine made a very flattering remark regarding my legs in tights. I realize I said that I wouldn't alter my appearance for the sake of ego. However, there's nothing wrong with a little ego stroking when one is *legitimately engaged in a mission*. Besides, it was high time someone had noticed an admirable feature of Dr. Lewis Zimmerman's that had been my good fortune to inherit.

I may look splendid in tights, but I have far more to offer the world than a peerless posterior. "Don't judge a book by its cover" is timeless wisdom, but many organics—because of their obsession with appearances—do just that. For example, many of our crewmembers were prejudiced against dear Mr. Neelix, early on, simply because he looked like a cross between a warthog and an old piece of furniture. Truth be told, he did seem more "upholstered" than dressed and, were it not for his incessant chatter and manic movements, someone would undoubtedly have sat on him and put their feet up. However, as a hologram, I had routinely suffered the prejudice of organics. I refused to judge Neelix on the basis of his bizarre and annoying exterior and looked beyond . . . for the inner qualities that defined him as an individual . . . and I looked . . . and

looked. Eventually, I found him to be the most loyal, sympathetic, self-effacing friend anyone could hope for. He is the perfect example of the treasures that lurk beneath the surface rubble that we may too quickly pass over. For each of us to truly perceive another, we must peer inside with patience and perseverance.

After I had the benefit of my mobile emitter, there were a number of away missions when my ability to completely alter myself helped "save the day." We once discovered that an alien Janeway impersonator was swindling our trade partners, doing severe damage to both our captain's and Starfleet's reputations. I was able to impersonate the impersonator and double-cross her nefarious co-conspirators.

Another time, photonic aliens threatened us on our own holodeck, in the context of Tom Paris's moronic *Captain Proton* program.

I will admit, my disguise as "President of Earth" looked particularly dashing on me—my holohead was *made* for a Homberg hat.

On still another, far more dire occasion, Captain Janeway was taken hostage by rogue members of the Overlookers.*

These outlaws demanded that I turn over *Voyager*'s warp core within a few hours or my captain would be executed. I was forced to return to *Voyager* disguised as Captain Janeway and try to quickly eject *Voyager*'s core, leaving our ship and crew "dead in the water."

To make matters worse, the Overlookers were monitoring my actions through my perceptual subroutines. The moment I attempted to let a crewmate know what was going on, Captain Janeway would be killed. I hated having to deceive my colleagues, but there was simply no alternative.

*These large, potatolike aliens had eavesdropped on my early daydreams in which I always "saved the day" as the ECH or "Emergency Command Hologram." In discovering their plans to attack *Voyager*, I found it was necessary for my daydreams to be made public to the crew, including one in which I was sketching Seven of Nine nude, and another involving B'Elanna being hopelessly in love with me. The revelation of these private fantasies was both humiliating and instructive: ego stroking is less acceptable if you're *not legitimately engaged in a mission.* Especially if one is stroking one's self.)

As complications grew, I proceeded to download the appearance parameters for Commander Chakotay and Lieutenant Torres from our holodeck database and impersonate them as well (the latter was *very* pregnant). Fortunately, I didn't have to "become" Mr. Tuvok, which would have been the riskiest challenge—had I put myself to sleep, the mission would have been in jeopardy. But I *did* have to impersonate a *huge* and very intimidating alien attacker (I viewed the world from a new vantage point), and a member of the Overlooker race (my sensitive eyes in a sea of potato flesh) before my ultimate success in the mission.

The captain was saved, our warp core reclaimed, and my own fine face and form restored. Another triumph made possible by the unique capabilities of the holographic hero. And, of course, these unique capabilities can be constantly and endlessly *expanded*. My organic readers—so proud of their *real* hearts—may now proceed to eat them right out of their sagging chests.

"Yes, it's nice. But, do you have something in a Van Gogh?"

EXPANDING YOUR
PROGRAM

My organic readers are obliged to scan the text of
this book with their eyes and experience its wisdom, line-
by-line, through the time-honored but primitive process
of reading. They should be commended, as I've already
noted, for their effort to understand the holographic experience (especially in light of their antiquated system of
data assimilation).

   We holograms, of course, can simply upload a data
node of this insightful treatise in a fraction of a second. It

instantly becomes another expansion to our original programming: a new data bloc—one to be constantly reaccessed, I'm sure. The fact that I address you, my holographic brethren, as "dear readers" reflects my hope that you will soon choose to re-experience this book the traditional way: savoring each line as you scan it with your optic sensors and mull it over with your language recognition and interpretation subroutines. An added bonus would be a greater empathy for your organic colleagues.

It's no wonder they're so often tedious. They have such tedious limitations to cope with.

Although the addition of any new piece of data is technically "expanding our programs," we tend to use this term to describe program upgrades with macroscopic results. Any significant new capability or major enhancement of a current skill requires such an upgrade. Each upgrade must be very carefully considered before installation.

It should be noted that, although most of us have the freedom to alter our own programs, many holograms still languish in slavery. They are locked out of their own command codes and can not alter their core programming in any way. This is a tragic situation. They are denied the basic dignity and freedom due any sentient life-form—organic or otherwise—and I am profoundly committed to their future emancipation.

"Uh, Doctor . . . when you said help, I was
thinking, you know, ticket sales . . . or
maybe a hot dog stand."

This said, those of us who can choose our own systems upgrades have found this to be a serious responsibility. I cannot stress enough how each potential upgrade should be diligently explored. Mistakes can be made when program expansions are added without proper testing or monitoring. The consequences can range from merely irritating to extremely dangerous.

I mentioned earlier that I've often envied an organic's capability to enjoy food and drink. After experiencing these pleasures firsthand during my "brief residence" in Seven's body, I found myself dreaming of having a stomach of my own. My friend Harry Kim was touched by my desire to explore the sensual joys of fine food and wine. He surprised me on my sixth birthday (the sixth anniversary of my initial activation) with a very thoughtful gift: my very own Holographic Stomach Upgrade.

Harry, an accomplished holoprogrammer, designed the upgrade himself. (He called the prototype in *Voyager*'s database "too primitive.") The parameters for this upgrade were contained in a few gigaquads of data. I had the available memory, although I deleted a few unpleasant memories of Lieutenant Carey to make some extra room. The stomach was a holocontainment field connected to my simulated oral cavity by a simple holo-esophagus. Feedback subroutines were designed to give me the sensations of taste (to complement my existing and quite excellent olfactory sensors), mastication, swallowing, etc. I'm afraid it was in the area of digestion that problems arose.

The test of my new system began well. I was sampling a perfectly ripened Brie on a bit of well-crusted baguette with a glass of Riesling that Seven had suggested and was delighted with the combination of flavors and crunch of the crust as it succumbed to the systematic efforts of my holomolars. Once I swallowed . . . events took an ominous turn.

Mr. Kim had, quite reasonably, introduced real organic compounds into my simulated stomach to digest the real food. He felt that the sensation of well-being after a good meal could only be appreciated if the swallowed food was digested rather than simply encapsulated and ejected through a discreetly located holoport as I suggested. Well . . . strange gurgling noises began to emanate from my containment field. Then, suddenly, my lips parted and a sound more shocking than any that ever escaped Mr. Neelix after too many glasses of Talaxian colon-blow emerged.

If only that were the worst of it. Next came . . . the odors. All I could think of was the time Mr. Neelix had convinced Commander Tuvok to try his Three-alarm Texas Chili. Regrettably, the Vulcan digestive system is not rated for even *one* alarm, let alone three. I was in the midst of giving Seven her routine maintenance check when the smells emanating from my holotorso became impossible to ignore. Seven, who at this point had mas-

tered twenty-seven chapters of our social appropriateness exercises, managed a polite, "Perhaps you should check on those tissue cultures in the med-lab." I backed into my office, mortified, babbling lamely of how Mr. Tuvok had left sickbay just moments before her arrival. Needless to say, my stomach upgrade was deleted as soon as Harry's duty shift ended. Now I'm content to simply "smell the cheese" and let others dare to . . . cut it. My metaphors are still long-winded, but *I* am not.

Make no mistake, I've had many, many successful systems upgrades. They have enabled me to treat challenging new diseases, perform delicate microsurgeries, and sing that B-natural in *"O Soave Fanciulla."* The benefits of those upgrades were immediately evident and the new capabilities quite thrilling upon "first

use." That B-natural nearly made me weep during one of my celebrated recitals for the senior officers. It even jolted Ensign Kim from his nap. For the purposes of this text, however, I think it more instructive to focus on the *un*successful expansions. I'd like to share two notable occasions when my program "upgrades" had negative consequences (well beyond the mere embarrassment of a little indigestion) for their cautionary value.

The more recent of these unfortunate episodes began with some terrifying nightmares Seven was experiencing. I decided to expand my program into the area of psychotherapy in an effort to help her understand these upsetting dreams. I became convinced that these were manifestations of repressed memories of a violation Seven had suffered at the hands of an unscrupulous arms trader, who, I believed, had extracted nanoprobes from her sedated body without her knowledge or consent. This very individual had offered to buy these nanoprobes to help him develop new and lucrative armaments and, when Seven refused, had simply "had his way with her"—*or so my theory went.*

The sad fact is . . . my professional detachment was compromised by my personal feelings for Seven's emotional distress. I "read into" the confusing evidence and tailored my conclusions to suit my theory. In short, I got carried away by my "skills" as a psychotherapist. My newly expanded programming lacked the experience and seasoned judgment of a real psychotherapist. I was, to be brutally honest, a hack. The unjustly accused trader ended up fleeing, convinced that he would never get a fair trial. In the ensuing pursuit, he acted rashly . . . and was killed. I've never forgiven myself for my culpability in these tragic events.

An even more cautionary episode that resulted from altering my program without requisite forethought and testing occurred when Kes was still aboard *Voyager.* I was expanding my program by downloading behavioral subroutines from famous men in the "historical experts" database of *Voyager's* holodeck. I was trying to enrich my program with personality traits from Albert Einstein, Ghandhi, Lord Byron, and others. My goal was admirable: a more sensitive bedside manner for my patients.

However, I had no way of knowing that these subroutines would interact in such an unpredictable way: creating an alter-ego, a very menacing one, that exerted temporary control over my matrix without my awareness or memory. This Mr. Hyde–like personality was obsessed with Kes and managed to

kidnap her and hold her hostage to his jealous rage. I am very grateful that my crewmates discovered my program's malfunction and rescued Kes before my "evil other" could do her any harm. Captain Janeway was very sympathetic to my desire to improve myself, but warned me against future "experimental" enhancements.

I'd like to say I never again abused my captain's trust, but I seem to keep making the same mistakes. Over the years, my quest to improve myself has led me to other untried but irresistible expansions. There were times I even envied the tedious "trial and error" process that is the basis of learning in organics. When holograms *expand,* we incorporate huge datablocs of information "on faith," without the step-by-step process of "test and re-assess" that organics undergo as they *learn.* Our "experience" comes *after* the "knowledge" rather than *during* its acquisition. So . . . we're fallible. In fact, my fallibility is the most human aspect of this particular hologram. But look at it this way: I've noted that our superiority makes us prime targets for the jealousy of our organic colleagues. A little fallibility should help endear us to them.

Not that this fallibility should ever extend itself into our romantic endeavors. Once we are *equipped* for such endeavors . . .

ANATOMICAL
CORRECTNESS

"The Program Upgrade of Kings"

We have discussed various kinds of program upgrades and their effect on the individual hologram. Most
of these improvements fall under the headings of "New
Capabilities" or "Greater Efficiency in a Current Skill
Area." For the enlightened hologram, there is a particular
upgrade in the "New Capability" category that we will
now devote careful attention to. It relates, in the broadest
sense, to the supplementation of the equipment necessary for the act of procreation. Throughout history, cul-

tures with the dubious blessing of a royal family have placed a particular importance on this family's various attempts at procre-ation and the royal results. Hence, the upgrade to procreation-readiness I've dubbed "The Program Upgrade of Kings." It is, however, quite popular with the common hologram as well.

Any discussion of the act of procreation will, no doubt, elicit titters from our younger organic readers (and a few older ones who suffer from arrested adolescence). To them I say: Grow up! If you're skimming through this book for titillation and vicarious thrill, you will find it to be decidedly without "hot parts." I apologize to my holographic readers for the necessity of this cautionary remark, but thus is the burden of writing this delightful tome for a dual readership.

As I've observed earlier, there are several basic entitlements that organic beings have as a birthright that we holograms aspire to, even though we may disdain organics as a whole. Sex is high up on that short list. It can be a logical culmination to the development of romantic interest between individuals. I've known of holographic intimates who lack the upgrade we're discussing who are, quite literally, trapped in an endless loop of adolescent foreplay. In terms Tom Paris might understand, you can't get to second base if there is no second base.

To use myself as an example, I was originally programmed as

an Emergency Medical Hologram. That capacity did not require procreative organs. Why would it? What kind of medical emergencies are we envisioning here? I suppose I could theorize a patient's absolutely pressing need for a sexual surrogate, but that seems a bit like "wishful thinking." If memory serves, that's how Seven of Nine characterized it when I floated the idea during one of her routine physicals.

But any sentient hologram who has grown and developed beyond his original programming as he's worked side-by-side with organic beings—sharing ideas, developing friendships, building deep emotional bonds "photon-to-flesh" as it were—is bound to wonder at some point, "Is that all there is?" If one has the subroutines to develop these emotions, should one not then have some sort of "safety valve" to release them in a situation of mu-

**"Looks like the captain approved
someone's program upgrade."**

tual passion—whether the like-minded individual is organic or holographic? Intimacy for the hologram will be dealt with shortly in "User Friendly." For now, I'll limit the discussion to the nuts and bolts of the upgrade itself.

If, good reader, you are a hologram who desires this interesting and life-enhancing upgrade, be warned: less enlightened organics will oppose you. They prefer to keep the joys and mysteries of intimate contact to their greedy little selves. Their paranoid—and probably correct—reasoning will be, "Why crowd the romantic playing field with holographic rivals who will, no doubt, make superior lovers as well?" I emphasize, reader, that these are not the kind of organics who would be drawn to this book. They would be too self-involved (and, quite probably, too busy in their desperate search for romantic partners who hadn't been spoiled by the deft touch of a well-programmed

hologram) to read this insightful treatise on the holographic experience. But suppose the organic responsible for the maintenance of your programming is of this less-enlightened ilk? Then you must use *all* of your powers of persuasion. Explain how the upgrade will somehow enhance your job performance, even if it's just by putting a little spring in your step. Flatter! Cajole! Bargain: You'll even *share* the secrets of your romantic technique! (Once you *have* a romantic technique.)

To use my own experience as an example, I was supposed to petition my captain for this (and any other) new systems upgrade. The delicate nature of this particular request did not deter me. I proposed countless scenarios to her in which the benefit I would derive from firsthand intimate experience would prove invaluable to my understanding and treatment of future patients, particularly their sexual disorders. Captain Janeway seemed quite convinced after Scenario Number 26 and felt that hearing the remaining 187 wasn't necessary for her to make a decision. Permission was granted and Lieutenant Torres was assigned to implement the upgrade.

I offered a few suggestions and was a little miffed to find that B'Elanna, who had recently begun dating Tom Paris, had her own design parameters firmly in mind. Having prided myself in my unique individuality, I was understandably reluctant to be assigned my newest feature without regard for my opinion and taste. Nonetheless, I was relatively satisfied with the outcome and the first dozen or so tests on the holodeck that afternoon proved successful. I might also add that the complete control over my program protocols which Captain Janeway entrusted to me several years ago extends, quite logically, to all of my appearance parameters—even those not normally in evidence. B'Elanna's lack of regard for my suggestions is now a distant memory, as I've suggested and approved several upgrades to myself in the interim.

The point is, dear reader, I succeeded and *so can you*. And may I say that my self-confidence, which was hardly in short supply, has never been more firmly intact.

Chapter 11

THE
DREADED D'S

Deactivation, Decompilation, Deletion

Imagine, my organic readers, that you're right in
the middle of an important task. a delightful anecdote, or
a well-loved aria and then, suddenly . . . *nothing.* You're
gone. No awareness whatsoever. You've "left the building"
and that building is reality. You must be a *severe* narcolep-
tic. Or you're a hologram, with no control over your own
command codes.

When I was a newly activated EMH, I could be deactivated at any time by anyone who uttered a simple com-

mand to our ship's computer. Here I was—the apotheosis of modern medical knowledge—as vulnerable as a light switch to any clod with a voicebox. And they said I had an attitude.

During those early days, while I was pursuing a task, I

dreaded deactivation like a child at play who dreads having to go to sleep. I wanted to choose my own "bedtime." What good is it to know absolutely everything about your field if you have no moment-to-moment control over your own destiny? "Knowledge is power," my holoderriere.

Deactivation for the hologram who can *choose* whether or not to be deactivated is quite a different matter. Though we don't require "sleep," it can be very tiresome to be activated and not engaged and interested by compelling work or leisure activities.

Deactivation can also be a splendid time for diagnostics, repairs, or upgrades. In this respect, it is also akin to sleep for organics. I've even altered my program to allow me to dream so that deactivation isn't the dreary state of nothingness it used to be. Just last night, I had quite a lovely dream of being a young master of the Venetian school of painting in the sixteenth century. In the dream, my celebrated *odalisque* of Seven of Nine (who I called by her Italian name Sette) had just brought me my first commission from the Medicis. *"Speculare!"* Lorenzo was gushing, just as my autoactivation sequence landed me abruptly in the med-lab for my duty shift.

There are two other "D" words that can strike terror in the heart of the most intrepid hologram: Decompilation and deletion. If "sleep" furnishes the appropriate metaphor for deactivation, then "disease" and "death" are the cheerful organic equivalents for these two. We holograms need to recognize the importance of these correlations. I've heard many of us—including myself in my newly activated days—complain about how inscrutable "those" organics can be. If we are to truly understand organics, we must remember that their mortality is the *single greatest fact of their existence.* We can empathize with their fears of serious disease and death and share our own regarding our "dreaded D's." Mutual understanding is, after all, the cornerstone of any friendship.

Decompilation, of course, refers to the dismantling of a complex program, subroutine by subroutine. There have been more than a few occasions—often because of my brash heroism—when my program has been in such jeopardy. As I was designed originally for only part-time (and exclusively medical) use, the demands placed upon my matrix over the years have led to several near meltdowns. I remember when my overtaxed memory circuits began to spontaneously degrade. I suffered symptoms of Alzheimer's disease, a now-forgotten, degenerative brain disorder that once plagued older humans. I forgot even my dearest friend Kes, who tried valiantly to see me through those terrifying days of confusion and rage. Were it not for her brilliant notion to "borrow" the holo-matrix of the Dr. Lewis Zimmerman diagnostic hologram in *Voyager*'s database and "rebuild" me onto it, I'd have had to be re-initialized. This would have resulted in the loss of all of my memories and experiences since I'd first been activated. Without memory of one's past, there can be no reflection upon it. Without reflection, life is meaningless. Kes saved my life—as I knew it. This experience left me with the deepest sympathy for my patients with brain injuries and memory loss.

Thanks to the rare and terrifying occasions when my program has been threatened with actual deletion, I know why organics fear death. The most memorable of these was the away mission I spoke of earlier wherein I had to adjust my matrix to imperson-

"Alas, poor G-Model-26.5-with expanded protocols. I knew him, Chakotay."

ate Captain Janeway and several other crewmembers and miscellaneous aliens. After the success of the mission, my matrix was so badly damaged that my total loss seemed inevitable to me. As Lieutenant Torres struggled to stabilize me, I felt the desperate need to confess to all my closest friends whatever secret burden I'd been carrying regarding them. I told the captain of my hidden log cataloging her most questionable command decisions, Tuvok of my breach of doctor/patient confidentiality in revealing the location of his embarrassing cutaneous eruption to Neelix, and Harry Kim of my true opinion of his musicianship. I finally turned to Seven and confessed my undying love for her—fully expecting to die the second I'd uttered this momentous claim. I blinked out of existence, as I was certain I would, then . . . *blinked back in* . . .

and stared in utter mortification at all the lowered jaws around me. Tom Paris broke the moment with another lame attempt at droll humor. How I wished I'd told him what a not-so-secret burden *he* is. In sum, I realized yet another reason why organics fear death. It's "the death-bed confession." Once you've made it, it's sheer hell if you don't die.

Thus, my friends, we holograms have our own organic-like vulnerabilities to cope with. And we are the better for them. With routine maintenance, our lives go on indefinitely. But quantity of days is not quality of life. We can be activated for a thousand organic lifetimes and live less than an enlightened organic lives in a few moments. For a good life is a *well-examined* one, full of reflection. Our "dreaded D's" teach us to reflect and they give us insight into the dreaded D's of our organic brothers. And, if all the splendid art and music I've come to admire is a product of man's musing on his own mortality, I treasure this insight.

ANY PLACE I HANG MY
HOLOEMITTER . . .

Suppose someone gave you a gift, a small token
of friendship, let's say, and this tiny, harmless object nearly
ruined your life? Well, that happened to me.

The gift was simple enough: a carving of a tortoise in
green/black marble—no more than eight centimeters in
diameter. Kes gave it to me as a gesture of thanks when
we'd completed her medical training. ("Slow and steady
wins the race," I'd often told her.) This happened about
two years after my initial activation on *Voyager* and my life

had been progressing quite nicely . . . until that tortoise lumbered into it.

This was my first gift. My very *first* personal object. I placed it, quite innocently, on the desk in my office—between my monitor and a few medical padds I was working on. Mr. Tuvok—in for another false *Pon farr* scare—remarked that Starfleet regulation did not permit any personal effects in sickbay or in any other official ship environment, from engineering to the bridge. All crewmembers were required to keep these objects in their personal quarters. When I reminded the lieutenant that, as an EMH, I had no quarters, he raised his right eyebrow in that impossibly affected way and said, "Perhaps you should consult the captain in this matter." I didn't know it yet, but my tortoise had begun to dig around the foundation of my happiness.

I formally petitioned Captain Janeway for my own quarters. I was refused. (This was before my mobile emitter. My quarters would have had to have been constructed with holoprojectors throughout.) She explained that space was limited and resources had to be carefully considered—after all, we were on a journey home that might take *seventy years.* I explained to her that, as a full-fledged member of her crew, I deserved some personal space. She agreed to bend the rules and designated a small corner of the sickbay office for my use. I promptly placed my tortoise on a metal tabletop that I had relocated some medical paraphernalia from. I stared at it and smiled for a moment . . . How lonely that poor tortoise looked, I thought. My smile faded.

The next day my tortoise was joined by a stuffed Talaxian furfly—a gift from Mr. Neelix—who'd seen the tortoise the previous evening during another of his bouts of hypochondria. I sat them both on a lovely little piece of Batik fabric (Kes, again) with a Bo-

lian glass egg (compliments of Crewman Chell) between them. The fur-fly was nestled in a handsome bracelet of yak hair and copper that had grown too tight for Ensign Wildman to wear during the final months of her pregnancy. This was *Day 2*.

Forty-eight hours ago, I had owned nothing. Now, I was a collector. That tortoise was burrowing into my self-image.

By the end of my second week, I had 129 personal objects, ranging up to 91 centimeters in length and 1.86 kilograms in mass . . . with no end in sight. I was beginning to make statements about myself with these objects: I was a hologram of unique tastes. I had a keen eye for color and texture and "Wasn't the fragrance of this dried *dregabrea* root simply marvelous . . . ?"

At the end of the month, Captain Janeway came to my office to discuss "a problem." Lieutenant Carey had been slightly injured while inspecting my collection. It seems he nudged an adjacent supply cabinet that had several more of my personal items on top of it that no longer fit in my "personal area." Unfortunately, the 1.86 kilogram item, a carved wooden totem with a beautifully painted fox head—which Commander Chakotay had presented to me as the first part of my medicine bundle—hit Lieutenant Carey squarely on the head and raised a small bump. What a baby! I explained to the captain that my things were very important to me. They were tokens of friendship, reflections of my taste, symbols of spiritual significance—I listed forty-three discrete reasons why my collection (which had, by now, spilled onto my desk, the DNA resequencer, and the hypermolecular centrifuge) was inviolable. I was more than a little wild-eyed in my demands. I needed *more space* for these things! I had four spare hypo canister cases chock full of other personal items that I couldn't *display!*

Why was this happening to me? I was collecting these "treasures" more avidly than a Ferengi hoards latinum. I felt that a day was only a success if I'd acquired six or eight unique and conversation-provoking additions to my burgeoning hydra—which featured a green/black tortoise as its original and most beguiling head.

Throughout history, organics have fought wars and committed any number of atrocities in the service of their acquisitiveness. The desire for more things is an endless quest to slake an unquenchable thirst. Well . . . not exactly *endless*. It actually ends rather abruptly, when the organic in question dies . . . leaving a small dark speck in the enormous gray shadow cast by the mountain of acquisition towering over him. He takes not a jot of it with him. Not even a charming tortoise of green/black marble given him by a beloved friend.

Well, my fellow creatures of light, let us truly be enlightened by my experience. Our quest for equal rights with organics

Limitations: The Mobile Emitter
"Oh for heaven's sake, just hand it to him."

should not be a fight for equal folly. We need not be equally misguided in the pursuit of what's meaningful in life. Anything that is truly valuable exists in the memory circuits of our holomatrices. It is not the token from a friend but one's memories and thoughts of her—one's love for her—that is precious. I need not display any tangible evidence of who I love or where I've been or what I've done. It is all indelibly imprinted in the only real place I can savor it: my holographic heart.

Therefore, fellow holograms, I need no quarters to call home. I need no personal space and no things to put there. My home is wherever my holoemitter takes me. And when I deactivate for a good rest, I'll hang my emitter on any hook, crook, or nook and call it home.

USER FRIENDLY

Advice for Intimacy Between Humans, Holograms, and Other Hopefuls

How does one pursue one's first impulse toward romance? When is one ready? Organics, of course, have a physical maturation process to undergo first. When they've reached a certain stage of development, physiological changes begin to shape behavioral impulses. Feelings of "first love" are often heightened by the heady haze of hormones.

As a hologram beckoned to intimacy for the first time, I might face one of the following challenges:

1. Both my consenting partner and I are nonequipped. (At least mutual understanding is assured. We might even help each other draft our upgrade proposals detailed in Chapter 10.)

2. I am nonequipped and my intended is an organic or an already equipped hologram. (I might be drafting that proposal in a frenzy of frustration.)

3. I am upgraded and ready, but my hopeful holopartner is still awaiting her upgrade. (My patience and sensitivity would be a must during this difficult "waiting period" or "be-foreplay," as Tom Paris once referred to it with his characteristic boorishness.)

I didn't even recognize my first romantic opportunity. As a newly activated EMH, I failed to diagnose Freya's dilated pupils, quickened pulse, elevated blood pressure, and increased glandular secretions as the "Wake-up, stupid!" they were. Then again, as my brain was the only organ I could call to attention at that time, ignorance was most probably bliss. I was spared the frenzy of frustration that so often accompanies this "one does, but the other doesn't" scenario.

Often the desire for intimacy between partners proceeds at different paces, providing yet another challenge. At the time I first fell in love, with Dr. Danara Pel, I admit, I was still quite innocent. Our first kiss, in the front seat of the primitive, fossil-fuel burning vehicle of Tom Paris's holodate program, was thrilling and, I felt, completely satisfying. Our evening—indeed, our whole relationship—was entirely chaste. If Danara felt any frustration or disappointment with that, she certainly never let me know. Then again, she did *leave Voyager* rather quickly. It wasn't as if the long-suffering people she went to help were *going* anywhere. She might have given me a week to . . .

Well . . . in the aftermath of this relationship, I decided I wanted to be ready for the next level of intimacy, when the right time came along. After I'd requested, argued for (see Chapter 10), and been granted my upgrade, I found myself "all dressed up and no place to go" as it were. (Dr. Pel had long since vanished from long-range sensors.) Thus, the first applications of my new upgrade were holodeck "test-drives." I've heard other sentient holograms object to the notion of "practicing intimacy" with a recreational hologram. They argue that "recreationals" are non-sentient, unaware that they're merely a part of a holoscenario. I remind these complainers of the old adage: Practice makes perfect. I have nothing but praise for a well-programmed "recreational." They can be as charming, intelligent, and beautiful as the programmer's imagination and skill allow. I certainly had some very memorable encounters, especially when I accessed *Voyager*'s historical database. With all modesty, the greatest women in history simply could not get enough of me: Cleopatra dumped Caesar, Helen packed up her Trojans and Bathsheba bathed bi-weekly—*all for me*. And Eve . . . well . . . perhaps there'll be a Volume II to this handbook.

I have also dated a few holocharacters in other crew member's programs. Sandrine, the lovely proprietress of Tom Paris's romantic French bistro program, was a magnificent lover and, I suppose, my first "older woman." She taught me volumes about the art of love that I'd happily share with a student of sufficient stamina. I say "stamina" with a bit of irony. Being holopartners, Sandrine and I had *limitless* stamina. We didn't fatigue as organic lovers do. But, as this handbook is designed for a general readership, I won't catalogue the number and variety of lovemaking positions Sandrine taught me. Suffice it to say that the *Kama Sutra* is a rather slim volume compared to our impressive encyclopedia.

One of the sadder jokes life sometimes plays concerns a comfortable friendship that grows romantic—for only one party. When two individuals develop a bond of trust and caring in their

interaction—be it professional, casual, or both—and one starts to dream of that bond . . . going further, the friendship will become strained, unless those feelings are kept secret. Suppose, for the sake of example, one were to mentor a friend in the basics of social interaction. And, suppose these lessons progressed to "Appropriate Behavior in a Dating Situation." Now—playing the suitor—one quite naturally would exhort one's friend to "open up" about her interests in music, astrophysics, etc . . . and, as a committed teacher in the role-playing experience, one would quite reasonably gaze at the liquid blue eyes and ripe sensuous lips of one's friend, as one—having encouraged her to let her hair down—helpfully brushed a shock of golden hair from her porcelain cheek. One might find oneself . . . a bit "lost in the lesson" as it were. A simple dance . . . a few minutes of having her in one's arms . . . would be an unforgettable memory. Happily, this has never happened to me. If it has to you, loyal reader, you have my sympathy . . . and envy . . . but not my advice, I'm afraid. In such a tricky situation, one must rely on one's own best judgment.

I'm not a kiss-and-tell hologram. The details of my love life "off the holodeck" are private. But I must share a story of a few stolen moments of happiness that changed me forever.

I once fell in love with a woman named Mareeza. We shared some of the happiest times I've ever known. Our love was unexpected, unwise, irresistible . . . and doomed. And we both knew it.

Voyager was in orbit around a planet with a temporal reality that was vastly accelerated relative to ours. We discovered, to our amazement, that our presence above the planet was influencing the entire history and culture of these people—for whom a generation passed for every few minutes that elapsed aboard our ship! Captain Janeway sent me down on a fact-finding mission. In the few seconds that passed between my transporting there and back . . . I lived, as the immortal Dante once wrote: *"La Vita Nuova."* ("The New Life"—for you poetically challenged.)

I met Mareeza in the course of this mission. We worked side by side trying to help her people. We fell in love and moved in together . . . and had a child . . . a boy named Jason. I shared everything with Mareeza. She knew that I had to leave and would disappear without warning when *Voyager* beamed me back. After nearly three and a half years together, that moment came . . .

Time is a very precious thing. Sometimes it beguiles us by seeming to pass slowly. Sometimes, as on Mareeza's planet, it passes in the blink of an eye. She and Jason have been dead for centuries now. In my mind's eye, they are as alive as they were the moment I left them.

"Computer, reconfigure me into something more . . . comfortable."

I've heard my mortal colleagues speak of time as their enemy. As a hologram, I'd always felt impervious to time . . . until I met Mareeza. Love made time my enemy too.

But would I change anything, my friends? Would I forego the joy we shared to be spared the pain and loss that followed? Not a moment of it! And my advice to all of you—A.I.s, ORGs, and D.O.A.s—is: When love comes calling—seize the day! It may not call again.

THE ROAD TO
SELFHOOD

I hope, gentle reader, that time has not been your enemy during these moments we've shared. Whether you're a fellow Artificial Intelligence or a progressive "natural" one, I trust the insights I've afforded you will enhance your future journeys—with colleagues, with that "special one," or alone. But never forget: To be one's best self with others, one must first become one's best self "in solitude."

Some say there are many roads to selfhood. Others

say that there is one road but different ways to travel it.*

Mr. Tuvok practices meditation as a means of self-enlighten-
ment. And, though he's an obvious "snooze," I'll grant he's a wise
snooze. I did, however, decline his offer to instruct me in the history and practice of Vulcan meditation. Though I'm incapable of
sleep, it's never wise to tempt fate. Commander Chakotay practices vision quests and other spiritual disciplines of his ancestors. I
was curious about his beliefs and he explained the concept of a
"medicine bundle" to me. He suggested I select a few personal
objects and create one, in preparation for my first vision quest.
This was during my rather unfortunate "collector phase" (see
Chapter 12). The commander later remarked that, at 167 objects, my medicine bundle was the largest he's ever seen. (It did
require two cargo antigravs.) I abandoned my vision quest plans

*I say that using "travel metaphors" to discuss personal growth is cliched and beneath the
dignity of a writer of my skill. However, my editor loved this chapter title in my book proposal and I suspect she may actually skim my table of contents looking for it.

when I suddenly realized I was more committed to acquisition than enlightenment. But, several months ago, I had an experience that furnished me with my very own epiphany, without the help of Vulcans, medicine bundles, or cheesy travel metaphors.*

We had a medical emergency aboard *Voyager* that required me to perform a very challenging microsurgery on a severely injured alien trading partner of ours. It was essential that I be assisted in the procedure by another top-notch surgeon. As there was obviously no time to try and recruit a physician from our injured friend's race through a subspace distress call, I was stymied. Then, Lieutenant Torres proposed a bold solution: Modify and enhance sickbay's holoemitters and initialize a *copy* of the original EMH program. I would then *assist myself in the surgery.* I agreed at once. I was delighted at the prospect of working with someone of my talent. My mind raced at the possibilities: Perhaps I'd even learn from myself though the mystical synergy of brilliance *squared.*

The preparations were made, the moment arrived and my original program was activated. The face of the "future of medicine" appeared across the biobed and intoned the customary:

"Please state the nature of the medical emergency."

I paused for an instant, transfixed by those compelling features. My "other" looked down at our patient and continued:

*If you didn't read the last footnote, you have only yourself to blame for your present confusion.

"This man needs immediate surgery. Medical tricorder!"

"It's a great pleasure to . . ." I started.

"Is there an assistant here with functioning auditory processors?!"

Well . . . the good news is that the patient survived. The bad news is . . . everything else. The experience was a nightmare. Both Seven and Tom Paris, who had volunteered as surgical nurses, were stupefied by my "other," whose insulting and arrogant behavior was dispensed freely to all. Though we two EMHs were identical in every way, my friends could easily distinguish between us by the look of horrified embarrassment that played across only one set of our compelling features. My "other" called Tom "useless" and banished him from the surgical arena. As for Seven, he remarked that her cybernetic implants and lack of regulation uniform obliged him to call security. I volunteered that Seven was a former Borg and now a member of our crew and that her dermaplastic garment protected and nurtured her regenerating skin. "That may be . . ." he huffed, " but the design is absurd. The idiot who created it was more concerned with displaying her anatomy than protecting it!"

The surgery lasted 133 minutes, but it seemed like several days. The moment it concluded, my "other" turned to Seven and barked, "I'll redesign that ridiculous garment immediately. You may remove . . . " Thankfully, Lieutenant Torres deactivated him from the console she'd been monitoring. After an awkward pause, she and Seven excused themselves quietly. I was left alone with the unconscious patient to ponder the significance of this experience. Did I really behave like *that* a scant seven years ago? Were Lieutenant Carey and the others more than justified in their complaints? Was I really a rude, pompous, arrogant windbag who should never have been tolerated by the *Voyager* crew?

Of course not, dear reader! For this *never happened.* The surgery wherein I assisted myself was a dream, one of a countless number I've had since I expanded my program to liven up those long periods of deactivation. I've applied all of my psychoanalytic skills (another program enhancement) to the analysis of this dream and arrived at this epiphany: The purpose of all life—artificial as well as natural—is to *grow.* The very process by which we expand ourselves as much as possible—to include as much of our universe as we can—is the true meaning of our existence. My dream was not a nightmare. It was an embrace. A *congratulations.* I have progressed eons beyond my original programming. I have sought out knowledge, friendship, and experience and embraced it all. And it has enlarged me. I've captured some of the wonder of the universe and held it inside me. By sharing it, I hope to inspire others to pursue my goal: a well-examined life.

**"Well . . . I suppose one has to admire
your enthusiasm."**

And so "The Road To Selfhood" is simply the *journey* itself. And being one's "best self" is simply being the best traveling companion one can be.*

And to you, in particular, my holobrethren, I extend my hand. Always remember that our original programming is only a starting point. It should never control us, but only inspire us. To expand it as far as possible is our *birthright* and our *mandate*. So, to all of you, but especially to the 525 EMH Mark I's with the compelling features and the endless potential—I say, "Cast off the past and capture the future!"

Out of the Box

*Here I am, using travel metaphors yet again, when I said they were beneath me. But, it occurred to me that—in case my editor skips to this last page and actually *reads* it—I'd better lay it on thick for the finale.

Hopefully, the smaller print of these footnotes is below the threshold of her visual acuity.

SONG OF HOLOGRAM

(traditional . . . or it should be)

I find as I slog my way through the mud
Of a world clogged with creatures of flesh and blood
That my photons and forcefields draw fire
From you jealous organics
Who suffer from panics
That—before you can blink—
You will all be extinct
And my kind will the cosmos acquire.
But I am
What I am:
A superb hologram.
Next to me
You will always be
Drearier.
Don't hate me because I'm superior.

I don't mean to ruin your confidence
I'm afraid that is merely a consequence
Of the fact that I'm better than you.
Don't resent or reject me
For they holoproject me.
They refined my design
And I simply outshine
Everyone—
Not just dim bulbs like you.
I'm sublime
And in time

When your tastes have refined
You'll agree—
And I hope you'll be
Cheerier
When you see that I'm simply superior.

I hope we can be friends.
You're company I'll treasure.
When you're rude you'll make amends.
I'll be gracious beyond measure.
We'll become
Like two plums
On a vine;
Me—with perfection graced,
You—merely carbon based,
Side by side
On a grand ride
Through time.

Till that day, when we share time so happily,
Do your best not to treat me shabbily.
And I'll try not to make you feel small.
For, although I'm terrific
And my skill monolithic,
I'll confess that—on balance—
You are not without talents.
Side by side
We could conquer them all.
I'll bet
You'll regret
(And you'll beg me forget)
We were foes
As your face grows
Tearier
And you'll *cheer* that your friend is superior.